The Spirit of Sw

Hamlin Garland

Alpha Editions

This edition published in 2024

ISBN : 9789361475740

Design and Setting By
Alpha Editions
www.alphaedis.com
Email - info@alphaedis.com

As per information held with us this book is in Public Domain.
This book is a reproduction of an important historical work. Alpha Editions uses the best technology to reproduce historical work in the same manner it was first published to preserve its original nature. Any marks or number seen are left intentionally to preserve its true form.

CONTENTS

THE MYSTERY OF MOUNTAINS .... - 1 -

Part I .... - 3 -

CHAPTER I .... - 5 -

CHAPTER II .... - 10 -

Part II .... - 17 -

CHAPTER I .... - 19 -

CHAPTER II .... - 25 -

PART III .... - 30 -

CHAPTER I .... - 31 -

CHAPTER II .... - 42 -

THE MYSTERY OF MOUNTAINS

As the sun sinks
And the cañons deepening in color
Add mystery to silence
Then the lone traveller lying out-stretched
Beneath the silent pines on some high range
Watches and listens in ecstasy of fear
And timorous admiration.

In the roar of the stream he catches
The reminiscent echo of colossal cataracts;
In the cry of the cliff-bird
He thinks he hears the eagle's scream
Or yowl of far-off mountain-lion;
In the fall of a loose rock
He fancies the menacing footfall of the grizzly bear;
And in the black deeps of the lower cañon
His dreaming eyes detect once more
Prodigious lines of buffalo crawling snake-wise
Athwart the stream,
Or files of Indian warriors
Winding downward to the distant plain,
Where camp-fires gleam like stars.

PART I

CHAPTER I

One spring day a young man of good mental furnishing and very slender purse walked over the shoulder of Mount Mogallon and down the trail to Gold Creek. He walked because the stage fare seemed too high.

Two years and four months later he was pointed out to strangers by the people of Sweetwater Springs. "That is Richard Clement, the sole owner of 'The Witch,' a mine valued at three millions of dollars." This in itself was truly an epic.

Sweetwater Springs was a village in a cañon, out of which rose two wonderful springs of water whose virtues were known throughout the land. The village was wedged in the cañon which ran to the mighty breast of Mogallon like a fold in a king's robe.

The village and its life centered around the pavilion which roofed the spring, and Clement spent his evenings there in order to see the people, at least, as they joyously thronged about the music-stand and sipped the beautiful water which the Utes long, long ago called "sweet water," and visited with reverence and hope of returning health.

Since the coming of his great wealth Clement had not allowed himself a day's vacation, and he had grown ten years older in that time. There were untimely signs of age in his hair and in the troubled lines of his face. He was a young man, but he looked a strong and stern and careworn man to those whose attention was called to him. He was a conscientious man, and the possession of great wealth was not without its gravities.

For the first time he felt it safe to leave his mine in other hands. He had a longing to mix with his kind once more, and in his heart was the secret hope that somewhere among the women of the Springs he might find a girl to take to wife. He arranged his vacation for July, not because it was ever hot at the Creek, but because he knew the Springs swarmed at that time with girls from the States. It would have troubled him had any one put these ideas into words and accused him of really seeking a bride.

He was a self-unconscious man naturally, and he hardly realized yet how widely his name had gone as the possessor of millions. He supposed himself an unnoticed atom as he stood at the spring on the second night of his stay in the village. Of a certainty many did not know him, but they saw him, for he was a striking figure—a handsome figure—though that had never concerned him. He was, in fact, feeling his own insignificance.

He was standing there in shadow looking out somberly upon the streams of people as they came to take their evening draught at the wonderful water of the effervescing spring. The sun had gone behind the high peaks to the west, and a delicious, dry coolness was in the cañon.

It seemed to Clement to be a very fashionable and leisurely throng—so long had he been absent from people either modish or easeful. He felt himself to be hopelessly outside all this youth and brilliancy and merriment, and he looked upon it all with a certain wistfulness.

He perceived at length that the strollers were not all of the same conditions. There were rough, brown cow-boys from La Junta and Cajon, and miners in rough dress down from the gulches for a night, but mainly the promenaders appealed to him with elegance of dress and manner.

Many of the ladies came without hats, which added to the charm of their eyes and hair. Some of them looked twice at the tall man with the big mustache and broad hat, who seemed to be watching for some tardy friend.

As he studied them his memory freshened and he came to understand them better. He analyzed them into familiar types. This was a banker and his wife from some small town—the wife fussy and consequential, the husband coldly dignified. This group was composed of a doctor and his daughters. Behind them came a merchant from some Nebraska town—he rough of exterior, his children dainty of dress and very pretty. Occasionally a group of college-bred girls came up without escort—alert, self-helpful and serene. They saw Clement at once, and studied him carefully as they drank their beauty cup at the circular bench before the spring. All good-looking men had interest to them.

All classes came, a varied stream, yet they were Western, and of the well-to-do condition for the larger part.

The deft boy swung the glasses of water on his tripartite dipper with ceaseless splash and clink. There was a pleasant murmur of talk in which an Eastern listener would have heard the "r" sound well-defined. There were many couples seated about the pavilion on the benches and railings. It was all busy yet tranquil. Each loiterer had fed, had taken his draught of healing water—and this was the hour of pleasant gossip and repose. Clement fell at last to analyzing the action of the boy who supplied the water at the pool. He slammed the glasses into the pool, and set them on the bench with a click as regular as a pump. Occasionally, however, he was indifferent. With some of his customers he handled the glasses as if they contained nectar, thus indicating his generous patrons. Once he stopped and dipped the glass into the pool with his own hand—a doubtful action—and extended it with a bow to a young lady who said "thank you" so sweetly that he blushed and stammered in reply.

All this fixed Clement's attention, and as the young girl lifted the glass in her slim hand he wondered how she had escaped his notice for a single moment. A woman at his side said sighfully, "There is that consumptive girl again, she hasn't long to stay." She was as pale, as fragile, and as lovely as the mountain columbine. Her face was thin, and her head shapely, but her eyes! They burned like rarest topaz—deep, dark and sad. Clement shivered as he felt them fixed upon him, and yet he could not turn away as he should have done.

He gazed at her with a sudden feeling which was not awe, nor compassion, nor love, but was all of these. He felt in his soul the subtlest sadness in all the world—the sadness of a strong man who looks upon a beautiful young girl who is dying.

Extremest languor was in every movement. She was dressed in dark, soft garments—very simple and graceful in effect, and her bearing was that of one accustomed to willing service from others. Her smile was as sad as her eyes which had in them the death-shadow.

Clement's action, the unwavering self-forgetful intentness of his look, arrested her attention, and she returned his gaze for an instant, and then turned away and took the arm of an elderly gentleman who stood beside her. She moved slowly, as an invalid walks when for the first time she is permitted a short walk in the outdoor air, leaning heavily on her companion.

The big miner roused himself and stood straight and tall, hesitating whether to follow or not—a sudden singular pain in his heart, as if he were losing something very close to his life.

He obeyed the impulse to follow, and moved down the path, just out of reach of observation, he fancied. As he made way through the crowd he grew aware again of his heavy limbs, of his great height, of his swinging, useless hands. It had been so long since he had mingled with a holiday company, he appeared as self-conscious as a boy.

Once the fair invalid turned and looked back, but she was too far away for him to discern the expression of her face. He was not possessed of self-esteem enough to believe she had turned to look for him.

He followed them in their slow pace till they turned in at the doorway of the principal hotel of the village. They entered at the ladies' door while he kept on to the main entrance and rotunda. There was no elevator in the house, and the invalid paused a moment before attempting the stairway. It was pitiful to see her effort to make light of it all to her companion, who was quite evidently her father. She smiled at him even while she pressed one slim hand against her bosom.

Clement longed to take her in his arms and carry her up the stairway—it seemed the thing most worth doing in all the world—but he could only lean against the desk and see them go slowly stair by stair out of sight.

"Who are they?" he asked of the clerk whom he detected also watching them with almost the same breathless interest.

"Chicago merchant, G. B. Ross. That's his daughter. She's pretty far gone—consumption, I reckon. It looks tough to see a girl like that go off. You'd think now——"

Clement did not remain to hear the clerk moralize further; he went immediately to his own hotel, paid his bill, and ordered his baggage sent to the other house. He wondered at himself for this overpowering interest in a sick girl, and at his plan to see her again.

He reasoned that he would be able to see her at breakfast time, provided she came down to breakfast, and provided he hit upon the same hour of eating. He began to calculate upon the probable hour when she would come down. It was astounding how completely she occupied his thought already.

He struck off up the cañon where no sound was, other than the roar of the wild little stream which seemed to lift its voice in wilder clamor as the night fell. Its presence helped him to think out his situation. He had grown self-analytical during his life in the camp, where he was alone so far as his finer feelings were concerned, and he had come to believe in many strange things which he said nothing about to any friend he had.

He had come to believe in fate and also in intuition. A powerful impulse to do he counted higher than reason. That is to say, if he had a powerful impulse to run a shaft in a certain direction he would so act, no matter if his reason declared dead against it. The hidden and uncontrollable processes of his mind had given him the secret of "The Witch's" gold, had led him right in his shafting and in his selection of friends and assistants—and had made him a millionaire at thirty-seven years of age. He was prone to over-value the intuitional side of his nature, probably—an error common among practical men.

Fate was, with him, luck raised to a higher power. What was to be would be; the unexpected happened; the expected, hoped for, labored for, did not always happen. All around him men stumbled upon mines, while other men, more skilful, more observant, failed. The luck was against them.

It was quite in harmony with his nature that he should be absorbed in the singular and powerful impulse he had to seek an acquaintance with that poor dying girl.

Dying! At that word he rebelled. God would not take so beautiful a creature away from earth; men needed her to teach them gentleness and submission. More than this, he had an almost uncontrollable impulse to go to her, and putting aside doctors say to her:

"I am the one to heal you."

He had never had an impulse to heal before, but the fact that it was unaccountable and powerful and definite, fitted in with his successes. He gave it careful thought. It must mean something because it had never come to him before, and because it rose out of the mysterious depths of his brain.

She must not die! The wind, the mountains, the clear air, the good, sweet water, the fragrant pines, the splendid sun—these things must help her. "And I, perhaps I, too, can help her?"

Back in the glare of the hotel rotunda, with its rows of bored men sitting stolidly smoking, idly talking, his impulse and his resolution seemed very unmanly and preposterous. It is so easy to lose faith in the elemental in the midst of the superficial and ephemeral of daily habit.

CHAPTER II

Clement was an early riser, and, notwithstanding his restless night, was astir at six. The whole world had changed for him. It was no longer a question of ore and amalgams, it was a question of when he should see again that sad, slender woman with the hopeless smile.

He had now a great fear that she would not be able to come down to breakfast at all, but as her coming was his only hope of seeing her he clung to it. Eight o'clock seemed to him to be the latest hour that any one not absolutely bedridden would think of breakfasting, and at four minutes past the hour he entered the dining-room.

The negro waiter tried to seat him near the door, but he pushed on down the hall toward a little group near one of the sunny windows, which he took to be the sick girl and her father, and so it proved.

His seat at a table next to theirs brought her profile between him and the window, and the light around her head seemed to glorify her till she shone like a figure in a church window. She seemed not concerned with earth. He was more deeply moved than ever before in his life, but he concealed it—the only sign of emotion was in the tremor of his hands.

He studied the sick girl as closely as he could without seeming to stare. She was even more lovely than he had thought. His eyes, accustomed only to rough women, found in her beauty that which was flower-like, seraphic.

Her face was very thin, and her neck too slender to uphold the heavy masses of her brown hair. Her hands were only less expressive of suffering than her face. The father was as bluff and portly and irascible as she was patient and gentle. He bullied the waiter because he did not know how else to express his anxiety.

"Waiter, this steak is burned—it's hard as sole leather. Take it back and bring me——"

"Please don't, father; the trouble is with me. I have no desire for food." She smiled at the waiter so sweetly that he nodded as if to say, "I don't mind him, miss."

The father turned his attention to the country.

"Yes, there is another fraud. I was told it would help your appetite, and here you are with less than when you left Hot Springs. If I'd had my way———"

She laid a hand on his arm, and when he turned toward her his eyes were dim with tears. He blew his nose and coughed, and looked away after the manner of men, and suffered in silence.

Once she turned and looked at Clement, and her eyes had a mystical, impersonal look, as though she saw him afar off, not as an individual but as a type of some admirable elemental creature. He could not fathom her attitude toward him, but he thought he saw in her every action the expression of a soul that had relinquished its hold on things of the earth. Her desire to live was no longer personal. She did all that she did for her father and her friends wholly to please them.

The desire to aid her came upon Clement again—so powerful it carried with it an unwavering belief that he could help her.

What was his newly-acquired wealth good for if he could not aid her? Wealth? Yes—his blood! He looked at his great brown hand and at his big veins full of blood. Why should she die when he had so much life?

Meanwhile his common sense had not entirely fled him. He perceived that they were not poor, and he reflected that they had probably tried all climates and all the resources of medical science; also that the father had quite as much red blood in his veins as any other man; and these considerations gave him thought as he watched them rise and go out upon the little veranda.

Clement was not a markedly humble person under ordinary conditions. He had a fashion of pushing rather heedlessly straight to his purpose—which now was to speak to her, to meet her face to face, to touch her hand and to offer his aid. Naturally he sought the father's acquaintance first. This was not difficult, for the waiters in the dining-room had been pointing him out to the guests as "Mr. Clement, the meyonaire minah." The newspaper correspondents had made his name a familiar one to the whole United States as "one of the sudden multi-millionaires of Gold Creek."

The porter had "passed the word" to the head waiter, and the head waiter had whispered it to one or two others. It was almost as exciting as having a Presidential candidate enter the room. Clement was too new in his riches, however, to realize the extent of all this bustle about him.

When he rose to go one waiter removed his chair, another helped him lay his napkin down, a third brushed his coat, and the head usher kindly showed him where the door opened into the hallway. It was wonderful to Clement, but he laid it to the management of the hotel.

There were limits to his insanity, and he did not follow the girl out on the veranda, but when Mr. Ross came down a few minutes later to get a cigar Clement plucked the proprietor of the hotel by the arm.

"Introduce me to Mr. Ross, won't you?"

The landlord beamed. "Certainly, Mr. Clement." He took Mr. Ross by the lapel familiarly. "Ah, good-morning, Mr. Ross. Mr. Ross, let me introduce my friend, Mr. Clement; Mr. Clement you may have heard of as the owner of 'The Witch' and the 'Old Wisconse.'"

Mr. Ross shook hands. He was not exactly uncivil, but he was cool—very cool. "I have heard of Mr. Clement," he said. He softened a little as he got a good look at the powerful, clear-eyed young fellow.

The landlord expanded like one who has accomplished a good deed. "I thought so, I thought so. Mr. Clement, let me say, is a square business man. Whatever he offers you is worth the price!" He winked at Clement as he turned away.

Clement began, "I beg your pardon, Mr. Ross, for taking this liberty, but I wanted to know you and took the first chance that offered. I have no mine to sell—I want to know you—that's all. I wanted to meet somebody outside the mining interest. I saw you and your daughter at the pavilion last night. She seems to be not—very strong." He hesitated in his attempt to describe his impression of her.

The father's theme was touched upon now. "No, poor girl, she is in bad condition, but I think she's better. The air seems not to have made her worse, at any rate. I haven't much faith in climate, but I believe she has improved since we left Kansas City and began to rise."

He had a marvelous listener in Clement, and they consumed three cigars apiece while he told of the doctors he had tried and of the different kinds of air and water they had sought.

His eyes were wet and his voice was tremulous.

"The fact is, Mr. Clement, she don't seem to care about living—that's what scares me. She's just as sweet and lovely as an angel. She responds to any suggestion, 'Very well, papa,' but I can see she does it for me. She herself has lost all hope. It ain't even that—she has lost care about it. She is indifferent. She is going away from me just because I can't rouse her——"

He frankly broke down and stopped, and Clement felt his throat swell too tight for speech at the moment.

They sat for a time in silence; at last Clement said:

"Mr. Ross, you don't know me except as a lucky man—but I have a favor to ask: it is to meet your daughter."

There was something very winning in the young man's voice and manner, and Mr. Ross could see no objection to it, and it might interest Ellice to meet this man who had stumbled upon a gold mine. "Very well, suppose we go up now," he said, almost without hesitation.

The girl was alone, seated in an easy-chair in the sun—her head only in shadow. The father spoke in a low and very tender voice, "Ellice, I want to present Mr. Clement. Mr. Clement, my daughter Ellice."

The impossible had come to pass! As Clement bent down and took her hand and looked into her eyes his heart seemed to stop death-still for a few seconds—then something new and inexplicable took possession of him, and he stood before her calm and clear-eyed. "Don't move," he commanded, "I will draw a chair near you."

Mr. Ross said they had been having a long talk, and she listened, smiling the while that hopeless smile. Then the father rose and said: "Where is Aunt Sarah? I want to go down to the telegraph office."

The girl spoke in the quiet, tranquil voice of one to whom such things have no importance. "I don't know, papa. A moment ago she was saying something to me, and now she is gone. That is all I know. Never mind; she'll be here in a moment."

"I'll be back in ten minutes."

"I am all right, papa. If I need anything Mr. Clement can call Aunt."

There was a pause after Mr. Ross went. Then she added in the same gentle, emotionless way: "Poor papa! He is a martyr to me. He thinks he must sit by me always. I think he fears I may die while he is gone."

Clement leaned forward till his eyes were on a level with those of the girl, and his voice was very calm and penetrating as he said:

"What can I do for you, Miss Ross? I have the profoundest conviction that I can do you good."

A startled look came into the big brown eyes. She looked at him as a babe might, striving to comprehend.

He went on, "Here I am a millionaire, a strong young man—what can I do for you?"

"I think I understand you," she said slowly. "It's very good of you, but you can do nothing."

"It is impossible," he broke forth in answer, and his voice gave her a perceptible shock. "There must be something I can do. If it will help you there is my arm—its blood is yours." He stammered a little. "It isn't right that one so young and beautiful should die. We won't let you die. There must be something I can do. This wind and sun—and the good water will work with us to do you good."

His voice moved her, and she smiled with the tears on her lashes. "It does me good just to look at you. You are so big and brown. I saw you at the spring last night. Perhaps I have come at last——" She coughed—a weak, flat sound which made him shudder.

She tried to reassure him. "Really, I have coughed less than at any time during the last five months."

He faced her again. "Miss Ross, I felt last night a sudden desire to help you. I believed I had the power to help you—I don't know why—I'm not a healer." He smiled for the first time. "But I felt perfectly sure I could do you good. I feel that way now. I never had such a feeling toward any person before. It is just as strange to me as it is to you."

She was looking at him now with musing eyes.

"That is the curious part of it," she said. "It doesn't seem strange at all. It seems as if I had been wanting to hear your voice—as if I had known of you all my life——" She tried to suppress her coughing, and he was in agony during the paroxysm. The nurse came hurrying out, and while he waited at one side Clement felt that if he could have taken her by the hands he could have prevented it. It was a singular conviction, but it was most definite, and had a peculiar air of actuality.

When she lay quiet he approached again and said: "I'll go now. I must not tire you. But remember, I'm going to come and see you, and I'm going to do you good. Every time I see you I am going to will to you some of my vitality—my love of life. For I love life—it is beautiful to live."

She gave him her hand, and he bowed and left her.

She lay quietly after he went away and smiled, a little, wan smile, which made her pallor the more pitiful. It was all so romantic and wonderful— this big man's coming. He was so unspoiled and so direct of manner. She had the hope he would come again, and it seemed not impossible that he might help her, his voice was so stirring and his hands so big and strong.

Yet she was beyond the reach of even the conjectures of passion. She had come to a certain exterior resignation to her fate. The world had lost its poignant interest—it was now a pageant upon which she was looking for the last time, yet she was too tired, too indifferent to lift her hand to stay it in its course even had it been within her power.

At times, however, she rebelled at her fate. There were hours, even yet, when she lay alone in her bed hearing her father's regular stertorous breathing till a great wave of longing to live swept upon her, and she was forced to turn her face to her pillow to stifle her mingled coughing and sobbing.

"Oh, Father, let me live! I want to live like other women. Oh, dear Father, grant me a little life!"

These waves of passionate rebellion left her weaker, sadder, more indifferent than ever, and as coldly pallid almost as if death had already claimed her.

On the night following Clement's talk with her she fell asleep while musing upon one mind's influence upon another. Perhaps if she could only believe she might be helped; perhaps he was sent to help her. It had been long since such a personality had stood before her—indeed, no such man had ever touched her hand or looked into her eyes.

He came down out of the mountain heights with the elemental vigor of wind and sun and soil about him like an aura. A man of great natural refinement, he had grown strong and simple and masterful in his close contact with Nature. The clay that might have brutalized another nature had made him a mystic.

There was something mysterious in his eyes, in the clasp of his hand. The world was all inexplicable to her anyhow. Perhaps God had sent him to help her just as He sends healing water down from the mountain peaks.

In thinking these things she fell asleep, and it seemed at once that she was well again, and that she was dressing for a walk. Clement had called for her to climb the mountains with him, and she was making preparation to go, working swiftly and unhesitatingly—and it seemed deliciously sweet to be swift and active once more. She had put on a short walking-skirt and leggins and was nearly ready. She stood before the glass to put on her cap, and as she saw how round and pink her cheeks were she hardly recognized herself.

She seemed to hear his impatient feet outside on the veranda, and she smiled to think how typical it all was of husbands and wives—and at that thought her face grew pinker and she turned away—she didn't want her own eyes to see how she flushed.

But suddenly all warmth—all flushing—left her. She turned cold with a familiar creep and weakness. She could not proceed. Her glove was half on, but her strength was not sufficient to pull it further. She could not lift her feet.

His steady, strong tramp up and down the veranda continued, but she was in the grasp of her old enemy. A terrible fear and an agony of desire seized her. She wanted to go out into the bright sunlight with him, but she could neither move nor whisper. All her resolution, her hope, fell away, and her heart was heavy and cold. It was all over. He would wait for a while and then go away, and she would stand there desolate, helpless, inert as clay, with life dark and empty before her.

"Oh, if he would only call me!" was her last breath of resolution.

Once, twice the feet went up and down the veranda. Then they paused before her door.

"Are you ready?" his voice called.

She struggled to speak, but could only whisper, "Yes."

The door swung quickly open and he stood there in the streaming sunlight of the morning—so tall he was he seemed to fill the doorway—and he smiled and extended his hands.

"Come," he said, "the sturdy old mountains are wonderfully grand this morning."

His hand closed over hers, and the sunlight fell upon her, warming her to the heart, but before she could lift her eyes to the shining peaks she awoke and found that the morning sun had stolen its way through a half-opened shutter and lay upon her hand.

At first she was ready to weep with sadness and despair, but as she thought upon it she came to see in the dream a good omen. It had been long since she had dreamed a vision of perfect health with no touch of impotence at its close. There was something of hope in this vision; a man's hand had broken the spell of weakness.

PART II

APRIL DAYS

Days of witchery subtly sweet,
When every hill and tree finds heart,
When winter and spring like lovers meet
In the mist of noon and part—In the April days.

Nights when the wood-frogs faintly peep—
Tr-eep, tr-eep—and then are still,
And the woodpeckers' martial voices sweep
Like bugle-blasts, from hill to hill,
Through the breathless haze.

Days when the soil is warm with rain,
And through the wood the shy wind steals,
Rich with the pine and the poplar smell,—
And the joyous soul like a dancer, reels
Through the broadening days.

—From "Prairie Songs."

CHAPTER I

This dream gave to Clement, in Ellice's eyes, a glamour of mystery and power—beyond the subtlety of words, and she met him in a spirit of awe and wonder, such as a child might feel to find one of its dream-heroes actually beside the fireside in the full sunlight of the morning. The fear and agony and joy of the night's vision gave a singular charm to the meeting.

It startled her to find she still retained the capability of being moved by the sound of a man's voice. It seemed like a wave of returning life.

Her heart quickened as she saw him enter the dining-room and look around for her—and when his eyes fell upon her a light filled his face which was akin to the morning. She did not attempt to analyze the emotion thus revealed, but she could not help seeing that he looked the embodiment of health and happiness.

He wore a suit of light brown corduroy with laced miner's boots, and they became him very well.

He smiled down at her as he drew near.

"You are better this morning, I can see that."

It was exactly as if he knew of her dream, and that the walk had been actual, and a flush of pink crept into her face—so faint it was no one noticed it—while it seemed to her that her cheeks were scarlet. What magic was this which made her flush—she whom Death had claimed as his own?

Mr. Ross invited Clement to sit with them, as she hoped he would. Clement had, indeed, intended to force the invitation. "I'm going for a gallop this morning," he said in explanation of his dress. "I wish you could go too," he added, addressing Ellice.

Mr. Ross introduced him to the elderly woman: "Mr. Clement, let me present you to my sister, Miss Ross."

Miss Ross was plump like her brother, and a handsome woman, but irritable like him. She complained, also, of the altitude and of the chill shadows. Neither father nor aunt formed a suitable companion for the sick girl.

Clement was the antidote. His whole manner of treatment was of the hopeful, buoyant sort. He spoke of the magnificent weather, of the mountains, of the purity of the water.

"After I get back from my ride I wish you'd let me come and talk with you. Perhaps," he added, "you'll be able to walk a little way with me."

He made the breakfast almost cheerful by his presence, and went away saying:

"I'll be back by ten o'clock and I shall expect to find you ready for a walk."

Miss Ross was astonished both at his assurance and at Ellice's singular interest and apparent acquiescence.

"Well, that is a most extraordinary man. I wonder if that's the Western way."

"I wish I were able to do as he says," the girl said quietly. The old people looked up in astonishment.

"Aunt Sarah, I want you to help me dress. I'm going to try to walk a little."

"Not with that man?" the aunt inquired in protest.

"Yes, Aunt." Her voice was vibrant with fixed purpose.

"But think how you would look leaning on his arm."

"Auntie, dear, I have gone long past that point. It doesn't matter how it looks. I cannot live merely to please the world. He has asked me, and if I can I will go."

Mr. Ross broke in, "Why, of course, what harm can it do? I'd let her lean on the arm of 'Cherokee Bill' if she wanted to." They all smiled at this, and he added, "The trouble has been she didn't want to do anything at all, and now she shall do what she likes."

It all seemed very coarse and common now, and she could not tell them the secret of the dream that had so impressed her, and of her growing faith that this strong man could help her back to health and life. She only smiled in her slow, faint way, and made preparation to go with him who meant so much to her.

He met her on the veranda in a handsome Prince Albert suit of gray with a broad-brimmed gray hat to match. He looked like some of the pictures of Western Congressmen she had seen, only more refined and gentle. He wore his coat unbuttoned, and it had the effect of draping his tall, erect frame, and the hat suited well with the large lines of his nose and chin. It seemed to her she had never seen a more striking and picturesque figure.

"I'll carry you down the stairs if you'll say the word," he said as they paused a moment at the topmost step.

"Oh, no. I can walk if you will give me time."

"Time! Time is money. I can't afford it." He stooped and lifted her in his right arm, and before she could protest he was half way down the stairway. He laughed at the horrified face of the aunt. He was following impulses now. As they walked side by side slowly—she, not without considerable effort—up toward the spring, he said abruptly, but tenderly:

"You must think you're better—that's half the battle. See that stream? Some day I'm going to show you where it starts. Do you know if you drink of that water up at its source above timber-line it will cure you?"

She saw his intent and said, "I'm afraid I'll be cured before I get to the spring."

"I'm going to make it my aim in life to see you drink at that pool." His directness and simplicity stimulated her like some mediæval elixir. He made her forget her pain. They did not talk much until they were seated on one of the benches near the fountain.

"Sit in the sun," he commanded. "Don't be afraid of the sun. You hear people talk about the sun's rays breeding disease. The sun never does that. It gives life. Beware of the shadow," he added, and she knew he meant her mental indifference. They had a long talk on the bench. He told her of his family, of himself.

"You see," he said, "father had only a small business, though he managed to educate me, and, later, my brother. But when he died it had less value, for I couldn't hold the trade he had and times were harder. I kept brother at college during his last two years, and when he came out I gave the business to him and got out. He was about to marry, and the business wouldn't support us both. I was always inclined to adventure anyway. Gold Creek was in everybody's mouth, so I came here.

"Oh, that was a wonderful time; the walk across the mountains was like a story to me. I liked the newness of everything in the camp. It was glorious to hear the hammers ringing, and see the new pine buildings going up—and the tent and shanties. It was rough here then, but I had little to do with that. I staked out my claim and went to digging. I knew very little about mining, but they were striking it all around me, and so I kept on. Besides"—here he looked at her in a curiously shy way—"I've always had a superstition that just when things were worst with me they were soonest to turn to the best, so I dug away. My tunnel went into the hill on a slight upraise, and I could do the work alone. You see I had so little money I didn't want to waste a cent.

"But it all went at last for powder and the sharpening of picks, and for assaying—till one morning in August I found myself without money and without food."

He paused there, and his face grew dark with remembered despair, and she shuddered.

"It must be terrible to be without food and money."

"No one knows what it means till he experiences it. I worked all day without food. It seemed as if I must strike it then. Besides, I took a sort of morbid pleasure in abusing myself—as if I were to blame. I had been living on canned beans, and flapjacks, and coffee without milk or sugar, and I was weak and sick—but it all had to end. About four o'clock I dropped my pick and staggered out to the light. It was impossible to do anything more."

There were tears in her eyes now, for his voice unconsciously took on the anguish of that despair.

"I sat there looking out toward the mountains and down on the camp. The blasts were booming from all hills—the men were going home with their dinner-pails flashing red in the setting sun's light. It was terrible to think of them going home to supper. It seemed impossible that I should be sitting there starving, and the grass so green, the sunset so beautiful. I can see it all now as it looked then, the old Sangre de Christo range! It was like a wall of glistening marble that night.

"Well, I sat there till my hunger gnawed me into action. Then I staggered down the trail. I saw how foolish I had been to go on day after day hoping, hoping until the last cent was gone. I hadn't money enough to pay the extra postage on a letter which was at the office. The clerk gave me the letter and paid the shortage himself. The letter was from my sister, telling me how peaceful and plentiful life was at home, and it made me crazy. She asked me how many nuggets I had found. You can judge how that hurt me. I reeled down the street, for I must eat or die, I knew that."

"Oh, how horrible!" the girl said softly.

"There was one eating-house at which I always took my supper. It was kept by an Irish woman, a big, hearty woman whose husband was a prospector—or had been. 'Biddy Kelly's' was famous for its 'home cooking.' I went by the door twice, for I couldn't bring myself to go in and ask for a meal. You don't know how hard that is—it's very queer, if a man has money he can ask for credit or a meal, but if he is broke he'll starve first. I could see Biddy waiting on the tables—the smell that came out was the most delicious, yet tantalizing, odor of beef-stew—it made me faint with hunger."

His voice grew weak and his throat dry as he spoke.

"When I did enter, Dan looked up and said respectfully, 'Good-evenin', Mr. Clement,' and I felt so ashamed of my errand I turned to run. Everything whirled then—and when I got my bearings again Dan had me on one arm and Biddy was holding a bowl of soup to my lips."

The girl sighed. "Oh, she was good, wasn't she?"

"They fed me, for they could see I was starving, and I told them about the mine—and, well, some way I got them to 'grub-stake' me that night."

"What is that?"

"That is, they agreed to furnish me food and money for tools and share in profits. Dan went to work with me, and do you know, it ended in ruining them both. We organized a company called the 'Biddy Mining Company.' I was president, and Dan was vice-president, and Biddy was treasurer. Biddy kept us going by her eating-house, but eventually we wanted machinery, and we mortgaged the eating-house, and the money went into that hole in the ground. But I knew we would succeed. I could hear voices call me, 'Come, come!'—whenever I was alone I could hear them plainly."

His eyes, turned upon her, were full of mystery.

"I have always felt the stir of life around me in the dark, and there in that mine—after we struck the spring of water—I thought I heard voices all the time in the plash of the water. I suppose it seemed like insanity, for I ruined Dan and Biddy without mercy. I couldn't stop. I was sure if we could only hold out a little while we would reach it. But we didn't. Biddy had to go to work as a cook, and Dan and I went out to try to borrow some money. I couldn't bear to let in somebody else after all the heat and toil Dan and Biddy and I had endured, but it had to be done. We took in a fellow from Iowa by the name of Eldred and went to work again.

"One day after our blast I was the first to enter, and the moment that I saw the heap of rock I knew we had opened the vein. My wildest dreams were realized!"

"And then your troubles ended," the girl said tenderly.

"No—for now a strange thing happened. The assayer tried our ore again and again and found it very rich, but when we shipped to the mills we got almost no returns. We tried every process, but the gold seemed to slip away from us. Finally I took a carload and went with it to see what was the matter. I followed it till it came out on the plates—that is where they catch the gold by the use of quicksilver spread on copper plates—and it seemed all right. I scraped some of it up and put it into a small vial to take home with me. When I got home the company assembled to hear my report, and when I took out the amalgam to show it to them it had turned to a queer yellow-green liquid. I was astounded, but Dan and Biddy crossed themselves. 'It's witch's gold,' Biddy said. 'Dan, have no more to do with it.'

And witch's gold it was. They gave up right there and went back to work in the camp. Eldred cursed me for getting him into it, and so they left me to fight it out alone. I was like a monomaniac—I never thought of giving up. I begged a little money from my brother and bought in all the stock of the 'Biddy Mining Company,' and went to work to solve the mystery of the amalgam. I was a good pupil in chemistry at college, and I put my whole life and brain into that mystery and I solved it. I found a way to treat it so all the gold was saved. That made me rich. I called the mine 'The Witch,' and it has made me what you see."

"It is like a fairy tale! What became of your faithful friends, Dan and Biddy?"

"I made Dan my foreman of the mine, and I built an eating-house and hotel for Biddy. They are with me yet. Eldred I bought out on the same terms as the rest."

He had a sudden sensation of heat in his face as he passed the chasm between the withdrawal of Dan and Biddy from the firm and his solution of the amalgam. He did not care to dwell upon that, because Eldred had sued him to recover his stock, claiming that it was bought in under false pretenses. Neither did he care to enter into the stormy time which followed the sudden leap of "The Witch" from a haunted hole in the ground to a cave of diamonds. He hurried on to the end while she listened in absorbed interest like a child to a wonder story.

She sighed in the world-old manner of women and said:

"And I—I have done nothing worth telling. I ruined my health by careless living at school, and here I am, a cumberer of the earth."

Some men would have hastened to be complimentary, but Clement remained silent. He was trying to understand her mood that he might meet it in a helpful way.

"But if I am permitted to live I shall be different. I will do something."

"First of all, get well," he said, and his words had the force of a command. "Give me your hand."

She complied, and he took it in a firm clasp. "Now I want you to promise me you'll turn your mind from darkness to the light, from the cañons to the peaks—that you will determine to live. Do you promise?"

"I promise."

"Very well. I shall see that you keep that promise."

CHAPTER II

It was rather curious to see that as she grew in strength Clement lost in assertiveness—in his feeling of command. He began to comprehend that with returning health the girl was not altogether pitiable. She had culture, social position and wealth.

The distinction of his readily-acquired millions grew to be a very poor possession in his own mind—in fact, he came at last to such self-confessed utter poverty of mind and body that he wondered at her continued toleration. He ceased to plead any special worthiness on his own part and began to throw himself on her mercy.

As the time came on when she no longer needed his arm for support he found it hard to offer it as an act of gallantry. In fact, in that small act was typified the change which he came ultimately to assume. At first she had seemed to him like an angelic child. Death's shadows had made him bold—but now he could not deceive himself: he was coming to love her in a very human and definite fashion. He dared not refer to the past in any way, and his visits grew more and more formal and carefully accounted for.

She thought she understood all this, and was serenely untroubled by it. She brooded over the problem with dreamful lips and half-shut eyes. She was drifting back to life on a current of mountain air companioned by splendid clouds, and her content was like to the lotus-eater's languor—it held no thought of time or tide.

That she idealized him was true, but he grew richly in grace. All the small amenities of conduct which he once possessed came back to him. He studied to please her, and succeeded in that as in his other ventures. He did not exactly abandon his business, but he came to superintend his superintendents.

However, he attached a telephone to his mine in order to be able to direct his business from the Springs. He still roomed at the hotel, though Ellice was living in a private house farther up the cañon. His rooms were becoming filled with books and magazines, and he was struggling hard to "catch up" with the latest literature.

If Ellice referred to any book, even in the most casual way, he made mental note of it, and if he had read it he re-read it, and if he had not read it he secured it at once.

"I know something of chemistry and mineralogy, and geology and milling processes, but of art and literature very little," he said to her once. "But give me time."

The highest peaks were white with September snows before she felt able to mount a horse. Each day she had been able to go a little farther and climb a little higher. Her gain was slow, very slow, but it was almost perceptible from day to day.

Mr. Ross had been to Chicago, and was once more at the Springs. He had brought a couple of nieces, very lively young creatures, who annoyed Clement exceedingly by their impertinence—at least, that is what he called their excessive interest in his affairs. Without the co-operation of Ellice he would have found little chance to see her alone, but she had a quiet way of letting them know when she found them a burden, which they respected.

One day he said to her, "Have you forgotten what I said to you about the spring up there?"

"No, I have not forgotten. Do you think I can go now? Am I really well enough to go?"

"The time has come."

"What would the doctor say?"

"The doctor—do you still heed what he says?"

"Must I walk?"

"Yes, to have the water heal you. But I will lead old Wisconse for you to ride down."

"After I am healed?"

"One can be cured and yet be tired."

They set off in such spirits as children have, old Wisconse leading soberly behind.

Clement was obliged to check the girl.

"Now don't go too fast. It is a long way up there. I warn you it is almost at timber-line."

But she paid small heed to his warning. She felt so light, so active, it seemed she could not tire.

For a time they followed the wide road which climbed steadily, but at last he stopped.

"Now here we strike the trail," he said. "You must go ahead, for I am to lead the horse."

"Not far ahead," she exclaimed, a little bit alarmed.

"Only two steps." He was a little amused at her. "Just so I will not tread on your heels."

"You needn't laugh. I know they hunt bears up here."

They climbed for some time in comparative silence.

"Oh, how much greener it is up here!" she exclaimed at last, looking around, her eyes bright with excitement.

He smiled indulgently. "You tourists think you know Colorado when you've crossed it once on the railway. This is the Colorado which you seldom see."

She was in rapture over the glory of color, the waving grasses of smooth hillsides, and the radiant dapple of light and shadow beneath the groves of vivid yellow aspens. The cactus and Spanish dagger, and the ever-present sage bush of the lower levels, had disappeared, crow's-foot and blue-joint grasses swung in the wind. The bright flame of the painted cup and the purple of the asters still lighted up the aisles of the pines in sheltered places.

"There are many more in August," he explained. "The frost has swept them all away."

"Is this our stream?" she asked.

"Yes, we cross it many times."

"How small it is."

"Are you tired?"

"Not at all."

He came close to her to listen to her breathing. "You must not do too much. If you find yourself out of breath stop and ride."

"I want to be cured."

He laughed. "By the way you lead up this trail I don't think you need medicine. I never finish wondering whether you are the same girl I met first——"

She flashed a glance back at him. "I'm not. I'm another person."

"That shows what three months of this climate will do."

"Climate did not do it."

"What did?"

"You did." She kept marching steadily forward, her head held very straight indeed.

"I wish you would wait a moment," he pleaded.

"I am very thirsty—I want to reach the spring."

"But, dear girl, you can't keep this up."

"Can't I? Watch me and see."

She seemed possessed of some miraculous staff, for she mounted the steep trail as lightly as a fawn. Clement was in an agony of apprehension lest she should overdo and fall fainting in the path. This ecstasy of activity was most dangerously persistent.

It was past noon when they came out of the aspens and pines into the little smooth slope of meadow which lay between the low peaks which were already crusted with snow. In the midst of the orange and purple and red of the grasses lay a deep, dark pool of water—as beautiful as her eyes, it seemed to him.

"Here is the spring," Clement called to the girl.

"I knew it," she said.

"Wait," he called again. "I must drink with you."

He hastened up and dipped a cup into the water and handed it to her.

"Now drink confusion to disease."

"Confusion!" She drank. "Oh, isn't it sweet? I never knew before how good water was. But here, drink. You are dying of thirst, too." She handed him the cup.

"I want to drink to some purpose also," he said, and there was no need of further words, but he went on, his full heart giving eloquence to his lips, "I want to pledge my life to your service—my life and all I am."

She grew a little pale. This intensity of emotion awed her as the majestic in Nature affects great souls. "I don't think you ought. I don't think I am quite worthy."

"Let me be judge of that." He spoke quickly and almost sharply. "Shall I drink?"

She had walked on while Clement was speaking, and stood leaning against the browsing horse. After a little hesitation she answered, "If you are thirsty."

The words were light, but he understood her. He drank and then came straight toward her.

She shrank from him in sudden timidity and said a little hurriedly, "Help me into the saddle. I shall need to ride back."

PART III

WESTWARD VISTA

The half-sunk sun
Burns through the dusty-crimson sky;
Streamers of gold and green soar
In radiating splendor, like the spokes
Of God's unmeasurable chariot-wheels
Half-hid and vanishing.
Around me is coolness, ripeness and repose;
The smell of gathered grain and fruits,
And the musky breath of melons fills the air.
The very dust is fruity, and the click
Of locusts' wings is like the close
Of gates upon great stores of wheat.
The gathered barley bleaches in shock,
The corn breathes on me from the west,
And the sky-line widens on and on
Until I see the waves of yellow-green
Break on the hills that face the snow and lilac peaks
Of Colorado's mountains.

CHAPTER I

At first Clement's happiness had no further base of uneasiness than the lover's fear of loss. It all seemed too good to be true, and he had a hidden fear that something might happen to set him back where he was before she came. It was quite like his feeling about his mine—it took him a certain length of time before he ceased to dream of its sudden loss, and now it seemed (when absent from her) that it would be easy for something to rob him of this love which was his life.

This feeling was mixed, too, with a feeling of his unworthiness, which deepened the more closely he studied her. She was so free from all bruise and stain of life's battle. There were no questionable places in her life. Could he say as much?

Whenever he asked himself the question his dealings with the stockholders of "The Biddy" came into his mind. Could he afford to tell his bride all the facts in the case? This feeling of dissatisfaction with himself led him to do many extravagant things. He presented her with beautiful and costly jewels for which she had little taste.

"Why, Richard. What made you think of that?" she said once after he had slipped away to the city to buy her something.

"Is it so very pretty?"

"It is beautiful! But can we afford such things?"

"We can afford anything that will make you happy."

He made a similar answer when she drew back a little startled at the cost of the house he had contracted for.

"Why, it is a palace!"

"The best is scarcely good enough for you." After a moment he added, "You see, I know you can never live East again, and I want you to have all the comforts of a palace out here. And so long as 'The Witch' holds out you shall have your heart's desire."

Mr. Ross had come to have a profound respect for his future son-in-law. "I can't say that he don't make as much of a fool of himself as any prospective bridegroom, but he is a business man at the same time. He don't lose his head, by any means." He was telling his son about Clement. "He is devoted to your sister, but I went over to his mine with him the other day and it is perfectly certain that he understands his business. He is only reckless when buying things for Ellice. He'll take care of her and the mine, too."

Clement felt a certain incongruity every time he put on his miner's dress and went through the mine. "I'm too rough for her, too old," he kept thinking—trying to conceal the real cause of his growing fear.

He was not honest with himself. He fought round the real point of danger. He gave a generous sum to the library, aided a hospital, and did other things which should ease a bad conscience, and yet do not. He hastened the house forward, and passed to and fro between his mine, the Springs and the city in ceaseless activity.

The marriage was set for July, just a year from the time he first saw her, and the winter passed quickly, so busied was he in building and planning the home. He grew less and less buoyant and more careworn as spring wore on, and Ellice could not understand the change. He was moody and changeable even in her presence. This troubled her, and she often asked:

"What is the matter, Richard? Is your business going wrong?"

"No, oh no. Business is all right. Nothing is the matter." And ended by convincing her that something was very much wrong indeed. And she grieved in silence, not daring to question him further.

The self-revealing touch came to him in a curious way only a few days before their wedding day. He was in camp on a final inspection of his mine, and was walking the streets at night, silent, self-absorbed and gloomy. He had grown morbid and unwholesome in his thought, and the wreck of his happiness seemed already complete. He spent a great deal of time in long and lonely walks.

The street swarmed with rough, noisy miners. A band of evangelists, with drums and tambourines, occupied the central corner. A low, continuous hum of talk could be heard at the base of all other noises.

Being in no mood for companionship Clement stood aside from it all, thinking how far above all this life his beautiful bride was.

There had been in the camp for some weeks a certain sensational evangelist—a man of some power, but of unhappy disposition apparently. At any rate he had been in much trouble with the city authorities. He had been called a "hypocrite and fake" in the public press, and had been prosecuted for disturbance of the peace. But he seemed to thrive on such treatment.

Clement had paid very little attention to the man and his troubles, but as he looked down the street at the crowd around the speakers on the corner it occurred to him to wonder if they were the fighting evangelists.

He was about to move that way when he observed near him in the dark middle of the street a man and a woman.

"This will do as well as anywhere," the man said, putting down a small box. He wore a broad cowboy hat, and a long coat which hung unbuttoned down his powerful figure. The woman was tall and slender, and neatly dressed in gray. Clement understood that these were the persecuted ones.

The man mounted the box, and in a powerful but not very musical voice began to sing a hymn full of cowboy slang. His singing had a quality not usual in street singers, and a crowd quickly gathered about him. His song was long and not without a rude poetry. He began his address at last by issuing a defiance to his enemies. This would mean little in an Eastern village, perhaps, but in a mining camp, even a degenerate mining camp, it might mean a great deal—life or death, in fact.

"Now, gentlemen, I want to say something as a preface in order to know just where we stand. Some citizens of the town have vilified me in private and in the public press—over an assumed name, however. It wouldn't be healthy for any man to do it openly. The man is a liar—but I don't care about myself. It is a little difference of opinion among men, but some miscreant has reflected upon the good name of my wife. Now let me say that the man that says my wife is not a lady and a woman of the highest character, insults the mother of my children and will answer to me for every word he utters."

A little thrill of interest and awe ran through the crowd. The man's voice meant battle, and battle to the hilt of the bowie. It was so easy to prove a mark for desperate men, but there was no fear in the attitude of the speaker. He had come up through a wild life, and knew his audience, his accuser and himself.

His voice took a sudden change—it grew tender and reverent. "I am here to preach the gospel of Christ and Him crucified. I may not do it in the best way always, but I do it as well as I know how." Here his tone grew severely earnest and savage again, as he added: "But I shall defend the honor of my wife with my life."

His voice and pose were magnificent—lion-like.

His manner changed again with dramatic suddenness. He took the whole street into his confidence.

"I love my wife, gentlemen. She has borne three children to me. She is a good woman. A mighty sight smarter and better than I am, but she can't defend herself against sneaks and reptilious liars. I can. That's part of my business. I tell you, boys," he added in a low voice very sincere and winning, "they ain't no man good enough to marry a good woman; it's just her good, pure, kind heart gives him any show at all."

A sudden lump rose in Clement's throat. The man's deep humility and loyalty and apparent sincerity had gone straight to his own heart and touched him in a very sensitive place. He turned away and sought the deeper shadow with his head bowed in black despair.

He thought of the eyes of his bride with a shudder almost of fear. Could he ever face her again?

"Oh, God! How pure and dainty and unspotted she is, and I—I am unclean."

He saw as clearly as if a light had been turned in upon his secret thought, that the ownership of "The Witch" was in question. He had not been candid with her—he had been dishonest. He had not dared to let her know how he had secured control of that stock.

All the way back to the Springs he wrestled with himself about it. He ended by reasserting the justice of his position, and resolved to tell her at once the whole story and let her judge. He had in his pocket the deed to the house and lot, which he determined now to give her at once, and to make explanations at the same time.

This he did. He called to see her the following afternoon and found her surrounded with women and gowns and flowers. The women fled when he approached, but the gowns and flowers remained, and there was talk upon them till at last, in sheer desperation, Clement said:

"Ellice, here is something that I want to give you now. It is my wedding gift."

He placed in her hand the deed. She looked at it.

"Oh, there's so much fine print. I can't read it now. What is it?"

"It is the deed to the new home."

Her eyes misted with quick emotion.

"How good you are to me, Richard."

"No, it's precaution," he replied as lightly as he could. "We will have a home always if you don't lose it in some wild speculation."

She put her arms about his neck, an infrequent caress with her.

"How rich we are. God is good to us. And is it not good to think that our wealth does not come from anybody's misery? It comes out of the earth like a spring—like the spring that made me well."

As he looked down into her face it seemed lit from within by some Heavenly light, and her voice made his head grow dizzy. He could not tell her his story then.

He sat down and listened to her talk. She wanted to know what troubled him, and he was forced to lie.

"Oh, nothing. I'm a little worried about a—new piece of machinery." This gave him a thought. "I must be away this evening. I can't take dinner with you."

She was not one of those who worry with expostulations or complainings. She had a mind of her own, and she granted the same decision to others.

"Very well," she said, and she flashed a sudden roguish look at him. "Don't forget to breakfast with me."

He had the grace to return her smile as he said:

"Oh, I'll not forget. I've charged my mind with it."

His going was like a flight. His inner cry was this:

"My God! I am absolutely unworthy of her. I am big, coarse and dishonest—unfit to touch her hand."

His gloomy face and bent head was a subject of joke for the acquaintances he met on the street.

"Saddle Susanna," he called sharply to his Mexican hostler. He had made up his mind to radical measures.

As he sat in his room with his face buried in his hands shutting out the light of the splendid sunset, he saw her as she sat among her soft silks and dainty flowers. Her lovely eyes and the exquisite texture of her skin grew more and more wonderful to him. The touch of his lips to hers came to seem an act of pollution, almost of envenoming, as he brooded on his unworthiness.

He wrote a note to her on the impulse of the moment. The missive read:

"I am not fit to see you, to touch you. I am going away across the divide to make restitution for a great wrong I have done. If I do not I can never face you again. When I see you again I will be an honest man, or I—if you think me worthy of forgiveness I will see you and ask it to-morrow.

RICHARD."

He added as a postscript:

"I am well. I am not crazy, but I am not an honest man. I can't kiss you again till I am."

Upon reading this note he saw it would frighten her, and keep her in agony of suspense, therefore he tore it up, and rushing out of the house leaped into the saddle.

The spirited little broncho was fresh and mettlesome, and went off in a series of sheeplike bounds which her rider seemed not to notice.

He drew rein at the telegraph office, and there sent three telegrams. They were all alike:

"Meet me at the office at midnight. Important."

As he turned Susanna's head up the trail the mountains stood deep purple silhouettes against the cloudlessness of the sky. The wind blew from the heights cool and fragrant, and the little horse set nostril to it as if she anticipated and welcomed the hard ride.

The way lay over forbidding mountain passes ten thousand feet above the sea, and her rider was a heavy man. But Susanna was of broncho strain with a blooded sire, which makes the hardiest and swiftest mountain horse in the world.

Clement's mind cleared as he began the ascent—cleared but did not rest. Over and over the problem came, each time clearer and more difficult. He must that night give away a hundred and thirty-five thousand dollars— terrible ordeal! Ninety thousand dollars to go to an old Irishman and his wife—both ignorant, careless.

What would they do with it? It might drive them crazy. As they now lived they were comfortable. He had made Dan sub-superintendent of the mine, and he had rebuilt the eating-house for Biddy. Could they take care of the big fortune he was about to give them?

Ought he not to give them a few thousands—such sum as they could comprehend and take care of? Would it not be better for them?

Then there was forty-five thousand dollars to be given to a cheap little man—that was hardest of all, for he had come to hate the sight of the sleek black head of Arthur Eldred. Yes, but he had saved the day. He had put in six hundred dollars when every dollar was a ducat. True, but the reward was too great. A hundred thousand dollars for six hundred.

Oh, this was familiar ground! He had gone over it in a sort of subconscious way a hundred times, each time apparently the final one. It had been quite settled when this slender little woman first lifted her face to him, and now nothing was settled.

It was very still and cold. There was no stream to sing up through the pines, and no wind in the pines to answer should the stream call. Nothing seemed to be stirring save the pensive man and his faithful pony.

Reaching the upper levels he spurred on at a gallop, finding some relief in the pounding action of the saddle and in the rush of air past his ears. The moon was late, but when it came it seemed to help him, lightening his mood as it lightened the trail. The big ledges and lowering, lesser peaks lifted into the dark sky weirdly translucent, and their upper edges seemed smooth and graceful as the rims of bubbles. Solid rock seemed melted and transfused with light and air. It was all miraculously beautiful, and the sore-hearted man lifted his eyes to the heights seeing the face of a girl in every moonlit rock and in every wayside pool.

As he entered the office he found them all waiting for him—Dan and Biddy in their best dress, and Eldred with a supercilious half-grin, half-scowl on his face.

Clement nodded at him, but said "Hello" to Dan and "Good-evening" to Biddy. Conly, his trusted, discreet cashier, was at his desk, and the office was dimly lit with a single electric bulb.

Dan and Biddy greeted him cautiously, for Eldred had filled their simple souls with suspicion. "He wants to compromise. He's afraid of our suit against him."

As a matter of fact Dan would never put a dollar into the plan for a suit, and it had never gone beyond Eldred's talk—and yet he had made them suspicious. Dan was forced to confess that Clement was becoming an "aristocrat." And Biddy acknowledged that he "sildom dairkened her dure these days." They had always felt his superiority and refinement, and they rose as he entered.

He wasted no time in preliminaries. "Sit down," he said imperiously, and his face, when he turned to the light, was knotted with trouble. He sat for a moment with bent head while he strengthened his heart to a bitter and humiliating task. He began abruptly:

"Dan, you remember the time I brought the amalgam home in a vial and it had turned green?"

"I do. Yis."

"You remember that you gave it up right then."

"I did. I said it's 'witch's gould.'"

"Sure such it looked like that day," said Biddy.

"All the same, the thing which scared you put a happy thought into my head, and I felt then I could solve it." He lifted his head and looked around defiantly. "In short, when I bought your stock in at ten cents on the dollar I knew it was worth par, for I had solved the process."

There was a silence very awesome following the defiant ring of the voice.

Eldred was the first to comprehend what it meant. His eyes glittered like those of an awakened rat.

"Do you mean that? If that's true you robbed us, you thief, robbed us cold and clean." He sprang up. "I knew you'd do something——"

"Sit down," interrupted Clement harshly. "I'm not going to have any words with you. If I had seen fit not to tell you of this how much would you have known of it? Sit down and keep your tongue between your teeth." He turned to Dan and his voice was softer. "Dan, when I was hungry you took me in and fed me. For that I've given you a good position. Is that debt paid?"

"Sure, Clement, me boy, it was only a sup of p'taties an' bacon, annyway."

"Biddy, I turned over two thousand dollars to you, and rebuilt your eating-house. You thought that paid the debt I owed you?"

Biddy was slower to answer. "For all the grub an' the loikes o' that, indade yis, Mr. Clement—but sure we wor pardners——"

Clement interrupted. "I know. I'm coming to that. Now answer me. If it hadn't been for me wouldn't you have thrown up the sponge long before you did?"

The silence of the little group answered him.

"Would any of you ever have worked out the mystery of that ore? Weren't you all anxious to sell for anything you could get?"

They were all silent as before.

"I made the mine worth money. I discovered the secret, it was my invention. I paid you four times what you had put into it. The mine was worthless until I invented a process for saving the gold. I claimed it as an invention like any man claims a patent right. I believed I had a right to it—to all of it, and so I bought in your stock after I had solved the problem of the reduction. I say I believed I was right—to-night I believe I was wrong—it don't matter how I came to the conclusion, but I've changed my mind. I have come to-night to make restitution. I am ready to pay you ninety cents more on every dollar of stock you sold me at that time."

Biddy gasped: "Howly Saints!"

Dan leaped up with a wild hurrah. "Listen to that now!" he cried, with other incoherences. He shook Clement's hand and kissed Biddy. He praised Clement.

"Ye're the whitest man that iver stepped green turf."

Clement sat coldly impassive and unsmiling.

"Then you're satisfied?"

"Satisfied!" shouted Dan. "Satisfied is it, man? Indade I am."

"And you, Biddy?"

Biddy was weeping and muttering wild Irish prayers. "Dan, dear, do ye understand, it's forty-five thousand dollars apiece to the two of us. Oh, the blessed old Ireland! I'll go back sure. Oh, it's too good to be true—we must be dramin'."

Clement looked at the distracted woman with a flush of self-righteousness. He had been right in his fears. It seemed like to ruin the simple souls. He turned to Eldred, who sat in silence.

"What have you to say?"

Eldred sneered. "I say you can't fool me. These shares are worth seventeen dollars and eighty cents each. I want their market value, not their par value. I want one-quarter the present value of 'The Witch.'"

Clement's brow darkened and his eyes burned with a fierce steady light.

"Is that all you want? If I served you right I'd kick you out of the door and let you do your worst. I know if you sue that you can't recover one dollar from me. But I have my reasons for putting up with your insolence. I will pay you forty-five thousand dollars and not one cent more. The market value of 'The Witch' to-day I have made by my management. I have gone on improving the mine day by day. As it stands it is a new property. You were a quarter owner in 'The Biddy.' We capitalized 'The Biddy' at your own suggestion at two hundred thousand dollars, because we wanted it big enough to cover all values. When I render you your share of that I am doing you justice. John, make out three checks for forty-five thousand dollars each."

Dan and Biddy turned upon Eldred and talked him into silence, but he was unconvinced.

Clement refused to touch the checks, and the clerk said: "Here is yours, Biddy."

Biddy went up and took the slip in her hands. "Is that little slip o' white paper really worth so much?"

"Call at the bank and get your money when you want it," said the imperturbable cashier.

Dan studied his check, his face foolish with joy.

Eldred took his, saying, "This puts into my hands the means to fight."

Clement merely nodded. "You know my address." Eldred went out without further word.

When the door closed on him Clement's face lost its sternness, and he became sad and tender.

His struggle was not yet done. His mind was clear about the man who came in at the eleventh hour, but it was not clear with regard to these true-hearted old friends who had been with him from the first. He recalled the time when Dan's big arm had helped him to a chair, and Biddy had put the steaming soup before him—food worth all the gold in the world at that moment. He recalled her broad, kindly face, hot and shining from the stove; he remembered their struggles, their sacrifices.

"Wait a moment, Biddy," he said, as they called out "Good-night," and started to leave.

"Sit down a moment, and you, too, Dan. I want to talk over old times a while."

They sat down in stupefaction.

"Biddy, do you remember the money you squandered on the lottery ticket?"

A slow smile broadened her face. "I do, Mister Clement—and I remember I won the prize sure!"

"You did, and saved all our lives. Dan, do you remember the day we lost our last five-dollar gold piece in the grass?"

Dan slapped his knee. "Do I? I wore me hands raw as beef combin' the grass that day."

"Ah, those were great days. We had days when forty-five cents would have made us joyous, and here you are with ninety thousand dollars, and wishin' for more."

Dan laughed again. "Sure, that's no lie."

"It is, Dan Kelly," said Biddy. "I have enough—too much. My heart misgives me now. I'm afraid of it, sure. I'm scared to carry it away wid me."

"You're safe, Biddy; nobody will steal that check." A sudden impulse seized him. "Dan, you believed in me in those days—give me that check." Dan slowly handed to him the check. Clement took it and turned. "Biddy, you fed me when I was starving, and you pawned everything you had to 'grub-stake' me—give me your check." She handed it to him without hesitation. He tore them into small pieces.

"Dan, you are mining boss, and I make you both quarter owners in 'The Witch' with all I have, and share and share alike, as we did when we hadn't a dime. Now hurrah for 'The Witch.'"

Nobody shouted but the cashier. Dan sat in a stupor, and Biddy was weeping, with one arm flung around Dan's neck. Dan was turning his hat around on his fingers and staring at Clement's face for some solution to the situation. It was beyond his imagination.

Clement did not speak again for some moments. When he did his voice was husky and tremulous with emotion. "You notice I say quarter interest—that's because there is a new member in the firm now. She comes in to-morrow. I want you to see how she looks." He extended a picture of Ellice to Biddy. She made a marvelous dramatic shift of features, and a smile of admiration broke through the red of her broad countenance.

"Oh, the swate, blessed angel. Sure, she's beautiful as one of the saints in the church. Luk at her, Dan."

"I'm lukin'. She's none too good for him."

"Don't say that, Dan!" Clement protested in an earnest tone. "All you have to-night you owe to her. All the best thoughts in me to-day I owe to her."

CHAPTER II

There remained to him now all the joy of riding back to tell her of his purification of soul. His heart was so joyous it kept time to every happy song in the world.

The gloom and doubt of himself had passed away, but the wonder and mystery of woman's love for man remained. He felt himself to be an honest man, but a man big, crude and coarse compared to her beauty and delicacy. He marveled at her bravery and her magnanimity. Leaving Susanna he leaped upon a fresh horse and set off, riding fast toward the divide. The wind had risen and was blowing from the dim domes of the highest mountains—a cold wind, and he would have said a sad wind had his heart not been so light. As it was, he lifted his bared forehead to it exultantly.

He put behind him, so far as in his power lay, all thought of the great wealth he had given away. He was eager to pour out the whole story to her, and hear her say, "Well done, Richard."

Over and over again his thought ran: "Now I am an honest man. I am not worthy of her, but at least my heart is clean."

Henceforth she was to be his altar of sacrifice. All he did would be for her approval. All there was of his money, his inventive skill, his command of men, should be hers. She should regulate every hour of his coming and going, and share all the plans and purposes of his life.

"Oh, I must live right, and deal justly," he thought. "I must be a better man from this time forth."

In the east the pale lances of the coming sun pierced the breasts of the soaring gray clouds, and, behold, they grew to be the most splendid orange and red and purple. The stars began to pale, and as he came to the eastern slope where the plain stretched to dim splendor, like a motionless sea of russet and purple, the sun was rising.

The plain seemed lonely and desolate of life, so far below was it. All action was lost in the mist of immensity—men's stature that of the most minute insects. And down there in the pathway of the morning was the little woman of all the world waiting for him!

As he rode down the slope to the river level into the town the sun was swinging, big and red, high above the horizon. His long ride had made him look wan and pale, but he ordered coffee and a biscuit, and was glad to find it helped him to look less wan and sorrowful. He dressed with great care, then sat down to wait. At 7:30 o'clock he sent a note to her:

"I have not forgotten. When do you breakfast?"

She replied:

"Good-morning, dearest. Breakfast is ready; come as soon as you can."

He entered the room with the heart of a boy, the presence of an athlete. He was at his prime of robust manhood, and his physical pride was unconscious.

She was proud of him, and met him more than half way in his greeting. Her face was still slender and delicate of color, but in her eyes was a serene brightness, and her lips were tremulous with happiness.

She led him to the little table. "Now you mustn't call this breakfast," she explained. "This is a private cup of coffee to sustain us through the ordeal. We all breakfast immediately after the ceremony."

"I've had one breakfast this morning."

She looked dismayed.

"At least a roll and a cup of coffee," he hastened to explain. "However, I think I could eat all there is here and not be inconvenienced."

They sat down and looked at each other in silence. She spoke first.

"Just think, this is the last time you will ever sit down with Miss Ross."

"You seem to be sad about it."

"I am—and yet I am very happy. I don't suppose you men can understand, but a woman wants to marry the man she loves—and yet she is sad at leaving girlhood behind. Now let me see, you take two lumps, don't you? I must not forget that. It makes the waiter stare when a wife can't remember how many lumps of sugar her husband takes."

He felt his courage oozing away, and so began abruptly:

"Ellice, I have a story to tell and a confession to make to you."

She looked a little startled. "That sounds ominous, Richard—like the villain in the play, only he makes his confession after marriage."

He was very sober indeed now. "That's the reason I make mine now. I want you to know just what I am before you marry me."

She leaned her chin on her clasped hands and looked at him. "Tell me all about it."

He did. He began at the beginning, and while it would not be true to say he did not spare himself, he told the story as it actually happened. He concealed no essential.

"I rode there and back last night simply because I couldn't kiss you again until I had made myself an honest man."

She reached out and clutched the hand which lay on the table near her—a sudden convulsive embrace.

"Last night?"

"Yes, I've been to the camp since I left you last night. I couldn't stand with you—there—before all our friends, till I could say I had no other man's money in my pockets."

She took his hand in both of her own and bent her head and touched her cheek to his fingers. She was very deeply moved.

And he—though his voice choked—faltered through:

"I gave it all back, dear—I mean I gave over to Biddy and Dan their full share—they are equal owners with you and me in 'The Witch.' I tried to withhold some of it; it was hard to give it all back; but I did it because I believed you would approve of it. And now, if you will let me, I can call you my wife with a clear conscience."

For answer she rose and came to his side, and put her arms about his neck and laid a kiss on his upturned face. Words were of no avail. In his heart the man was still afraid of one so good and loving.

THE END